Nyiraneza and Isaro

Written by
Mary G Mbabazi

Illustrated by
Peter Gitego

One day as Nyiraneza was going to school, she saw a young girl seated alone by the roadside crying.

2

"What is your name?" Nyiraneza asked the girl.

"My name is Isaro," the girl replied.

"Why are you crying?" Nyiraneza asked.

Isaro replied, "I want to go to school like you do but I can't."

"I don't have friends," Isaro continued to tell Nyiraneza, "My family hides me in the house because they don't want neighbors to see me. I escaped today."

"Don't worry," Nyiraneza said, "When I come back from school today, I will bring my favorite books and teach you to read."

Isaro went back home happy. She had a new friend who looked like her...

Nyiraneza was sad after hearing Isaro's story. She was quiet the whole day at school and her teacher saw it. The teacher asked her what was wrong and Nyiraneza told her about Isaro's story.

When the school day ended, the teacher asked Nyiraneza if she could go with her to see Isaro. Nyiraneza agreed and off they went to see Isaro.

When they reached Isaro's home, they were surprised to see more albino children living there.

The teacher talked to Isaro's family about albino children and how they can grow up to be like any other children. She encouraged the parents to allow the children to start school.

A few days later, Isaro and her siblings started school. They lived happily ever after without having to be hidden.

ISBN: 978-99977-773-2-4

Email: furahapublishers@gmail.com

www.furahapublisher.com